THE PASSPORT
OF MALLAM ILIA

THE PASSPORT OF MALLAM ILIA

CYPRIAN EKWENSI

First Edition published in 1960

Copyright © 1960, 2023 by Cyprian Ekwensi

Coming Soon *The Passport of Mallam Ilia* the animated movie by Magic Carpet Studios. For more information visit http://iliathemovie.com/.

ISBN: 978-1-960611-00-0 - Paperback
eISBN: 978-1-960611-01-7 - eBook

Library of Congress Control Number: 2023905247

Cover Illustration by Nancy Batra

⊗This paper meets the requirements of ANSI/NISO Z39.48-1992 (Permanence of Paper)

052523

PROLOGUE

L ate in 1947, my train was gasping and panting up the steep incline that leads on to the Bauchi Plateau in Northern Nigeria. It was a chilly morning; I had been travelling third class for two days and two sleepless nights with scarcely any room in which to stretch my legs; I felt bored to death, and anxious to get the journey over.

My companions were mostly Hausa men, Biroms from the Plateau, a few Yoruba traders who cluttered up the train with their wares, and one or two schoolboys who sat at the far corner of the carriage, talking excitedly about their forthcoming holiday. In such mixed company, conversation was apt to be rather forced, and little remarks intended jocularly generally went wrong and got misinterpreted as insults. So, I decided to hold my peace.

But there was nothing I could do to relieve the boredom. I had read the novel and magazines I had brought with me; the scenery was too familiar to excite me, and my temper was in no state to be improved by any undue mental exertion.

As I sat staring before me, the man seated opposite me did a most unexciting thing. He took out a bag from under his seat, and, fumbling in it, brought out a small flat blue book. He looked at it smilingly for a time and then put it back into the bag and continued to stare out of the carriage window.

There was nothing unusual about this. The book was his, and presumably, he had paid his fare. But my attention had been drawn to his face, and, for the first time since the journey had begun, I really noticed it. It was the face of an old man, bearded, with weak eyes from which the tears ran down freely. Even in a sitting posture, it was easy to see that he was very bent, and that his limbs were shrunk. What struck me particularly was the man's uncleanliness. He was very dirty, his hands were cracked by the *harmattan*, that cold dry wind that corrodes everything lying between the Sahara and the Gulf of Guinea; his clothes were grey with dirt; his face looked unwashed. And yet that book he had gloated over was a passport.

I wondered by what freak of circumstance such an insignificant-looking man could have come by an authority requesting all concerned "In the name of His Britannic Majesty" to allow my companion to "pass freely and without let or hindrance and to afford him every assistance of which he may stand in need . . .". In my boyish imagination, a man who owned such a valuable document could not look like this. Why, it did not seem to me that he could even read or write down his own name. I was so intrigued by the situation that impulse suggested my asking him a question.

I was still debating in my mind what course to take, when someone interrupted me.

"Hello, Hassan," he said. "Going to the land of the tin mines?"

I looked up into the face of a dark-complexioned man in a dirty brown coat. His face was familiar, but for the moment I was too irritated by his intrusion to recall his name.

"I'm sorry," I said coldly, "I don't know you."

He smiled rather shyly and went on to recount my past life. "Don't you remember how we used to play together at Jebba, near Juju Rock? Don't you remember the day you left for college, how you were weeping for your mother, and Captain Plowman—our Education Officer—pacified you and gave you one bright new shilling; don't you . . .?"

"I don't," I cut in: which was a lie.

"Sorry then! I just thought—if you were going to the mines, maybe you could help me land a job."

I remembered him now. His name was Kofi. He used to tell us fantastic stories of the days when the first white men arrived in Nigeria. He could not be over forty, but his imagination so illumined these stories that for us they became real. I had heard enough of these tales some ten years ago and was in no mood now to recall them or to give an ear to fresh boastings. I ignored him and turned my thoughts again to the old man.

I addressed him in Hausa with the respect his age demanded.

"Greeting!" I said. "I pray all is well with you on this journey?"

The *Mallam* (a man of some education and standing)

looked up at me and his eyes widened with surprise as if he were not quite certain whether after two days' silence, he had actually heard me address him. I hastened to reassure him by adding: "I see that the Mallam has travelled far."

"It is even so," he admitted. His voice was hoarse with the cold and with disuse, and he wept freely. "I have indeed travelled far."

"Mecca?" I asked, recalling that the Holy City was a favourite tourist's spot.

"Yes, Mecca; and beyond."

He looked out of the window, as if the interview gave him some pain, and for a moment I studied him silently. He was indeed travel-worn: his clothes were in tatters, and it must have been weeks since his beard had seen a razor. Even the small cap beneath his turban was visibly frayed.

Kofi Usuman was striving to distract my attention with tales of his own misfortunes and asked me openly what chances he had of getting a job in the mines. I told him that that was a question for the Mining Engineer and once again faced the old man.

"What did you do in Mecca?" I asked.

"I went to pay homage," he said. "Yes . . ."

"And beyond?"

"I was with the army. Among other things I was their doctor."

"You were an army doctor?"

He smiled toothlessly. "I should have said a doctor of the mind, as well as of the body; in our own little African way, of course."

"I understand," I said. "They came to you with their problems, both mental and physical, and you advised them."

"A kind of medicine-man," he explained.

"That passport I saw just now . . ."

"Oh, that! I got that in 1927. It's twenty years old now, isn't it? Odd, how time flies."

"Yes," I said.

He nodded. "Twenty years…but Allah be praised, those years were not wasted. I nearly missed him."
"Missed him? Who?"

He gave a guilty start and glanced about him. "I beg for mercy, Mallam. I was really talking to myself. Would you like to see the passport?"

I was still rather puzzled as I watched him bring it out and open it at the page containing the photograph. There was certainly no resemblance between him and the man in the photograph. While the one was young and virile, the other was old and decrepit. I saw before me a young man in his prime, his head crowned by a gleaming white turban, his shoulders draped in a velvet gown edged with gold embroidery.

"You've changed a lot," I remarked.

"Twenty years is not a short time," he reminded me. "But it was worth it. I did not give my life for nothing."

"Give your life, did you say? What do you mean?"

"My son, you are too curious. First you want to see the passport; and now you must know what I am talking about."

"A student is naturally a curious man," I told him.

"Spare me the pain," he begged. "My breath is poor, I cannot talk." He looked over his shoulder, like a thief entering a strong-room, and his voice sank low. "Look at this," he said, and lifted his dirty robe.

I nearly screamed at what I saw. Beneath his robe, just under the heart, was a long, deep flesh wound. It had stopped bleeding, and the cloth had stuck to its corners. The old man quickly covered up the wound and smiled thinly at me.

"I cannot talk much, you see," he panted. "It will soon be over. I have also taken some of this," —he showed me a white powder— "just to make quite sure. I don't know what the English call it, but, when I was in charge of the army medical supplies, they told me that—that as much as will lie on a sixpence will kill a man in about eighteen hours."

He began to cough desperately. When he had re-gained control of himself, I asked him, "But why all this?"

"Nothing," he said, shrugging his shoulders. "I just want to die."

I was at a loss to know what could justify this double attempt at suicide. He was coughing again, and I looked at the passport. It described him as Mallam Alhaji Ibrahim Ilia, a man five feet six inches tall, with no tribal marks on his face, a man born in 1882, and travelling to Mandara, Marua, and Fort Lamy for the purposes of trade. The passport was signed by the Resident at Kano and dated May 1927.

"I can't understand any reason for your action," I ventured.

"No, you can't."

He smiled. I wondered why I had not noticed before that I was sitting opposite a dying man; a man who for no apparent reason had taken it upon himself to bring about his own death. His eyes had grown more glassy since the beginning of our conversation. He was restless, yet too weak to move about. Now and again a violent cramp seized him in the arm or leg, and he cried out with pain.

"You're a tough old man," I said. "You've been suffering quietly all this time, and . . ."

"Toughness has its limits," he retorted. "I wish I could tell you my story...I feel you would understand."

"Don't try if the effort is too great. But if it will help you..."

"It will. I must! I must!" he pleaded.

There were times when he appeared quite normal, but his pulse was very low, and his voice almost inaudible, so that often I had to guess and suggest and gesticulate before a nod of his grey head told me that I had got his meaning right. That was how we spent the few hours left between us and Jos. Towards the end, Mallam Ilia became very emotional, and I had to remind him that the time was short, and that if he excited himself unduly he might never complete his tale.

About twenty miles from Jos, he closed his eyes,

and invited me to go over the notes I had made on odd bits of paper so that he might be sure I had missed nothing.

Below is what I recorded up to that time. The original was perhaps not quite as coherent as what follows, but the tale is, in essentials, what Mallam Ilia recounted to me, and I have as far as possible preserved his personal touch; for that grand old man was a great storyteller, and a devout follower of the Prophet.

1
KANEMI'S DAUGHTER

SHANCHI

My name is Mallam Alhaji Ibrahim Ilia. I was born sixty-five years ago, at a time when a man was a man, and women were won by those who deserved them. As a youth, my life was wild, and there was nothing I loved better than a good fight, or a hard race on horseback. My parents were wealthy and saw to it that I got nearly everything I wanted without question: slaves, gold, horses, merchandise in plenty and the best company at Kano.

As I grew up, my parents began to talk to me about taking a wife, and in fact they sent me all the beautiful girls within the famous town wall, but I was not attracted to any of them. I prided myself on being a man and did not consider it gallant merely to "buy" or "take on" a wife. I wanted something more romantic.

One evening, we sat round a fire outside my father's house talking about brave men of the past, the prospects of the British bringing an army to Kano, who would oppose them if they did, and what chances we had of beating them back. In the midst of our heated discussion, we heard the clatter of horses' hooves. A company of men cantered up to our gate and drew rein. They were Arab traders from the Great Desert. Splendid turbans crowned their heads, and their noses were concealed in dust masks.

"Greetings while you rest!" they hailed.

You are welcome," I answered. "How is it with you? Can we be of any help?"

"Yes," sneered the leader of the group. "You can be of the greatest help, if you are not *cowards*.

At the mention of that word "coward", my sword-blade flashed out. The firelight, catching against it as I sprang at the speaker's horse, made it glisten dangerously. The great man reared backwards, and, with a simple movement of his riding whip, flicked the weapon clean out of my hand, and roared with laughter.

"A brave lad, truly. Ha, ha! A brave lad. How would you like to win the hand of my daughter Zarah?"

My companions, who had also sprung to their feet at the mention of that obnoxious word, paused and regarded my fallen sword with a surprise no less than mine. It was the first time I had ever been disarmed by anyone; so easily too—*and* in the presence of my friends and hero-worshippers.

"Get out of here!" I roared. "You and your daughter."

"Gently, my young man, lest I make you sorry for your words. How dare you speak like that to

Kanemi, Prince of the Tuaregs?" He looked at me with a piercing glance, and, for a moment, I thought he was deciding to ride me down. But he changed his mind, apparently, and yelled out an order.

"Maji, put Zarah down, and let them see her!"

One of the men in the rear rode briskly forward, and leaping down, helped another figure down from the same horse. She was clad in white, and her head was bowed. We could not see her face, but it was easy to guess that she was tall, though slight, and her movements suggested that she had grace and poise.

"Take off the veil!" Kanemi snapped.

The slave took off the veil, and there, standing before us in all her glory, was the most beautiful girl I had ever seen. Her face was so radiant and calm that I had a sudden inclination to throw myself down on my knees and worship her. Her eyes were downcast, with long lashes. Her lips were slightly parted, and though she was not really smiling, her teeth gleamed in the light of our fire; truly, as beautiful a woman as I had ever imagined in my wildest dreams.

"She is yours for the winning."

"But how?" I asked.

"That you shall know!"

He gave another order, and the man helped her back into the saddle. "Come to Unguan Kanawa to-morrow at nightfall, and I shall tell you. Your will have to pick up your fallen sword, and bring it along; and while there, remember to hold it more firmly."

He laughed tauntingly, turned his horse with a swift gesture, and rode away.

We sat far into the night after he had left, talking about Kanemi's daughter. Nobody seemed ever to have heard of the Prince of the Tuaregs; and as far as Zarah was concerned she was a mysterious princess. So excited was I that I was sorry the Prince could not have made our meeting possible that night. It was the most romantic thing that had ever happened to me.

Next evening, I saddled my horse and rode to Unguan Kanawa. It was a little village some five miles outside the walls of Kano, and in the midst of it was a large mud building, decorated with flags and humming with music. Obviously, some big sport was in progress, and the man at the gate knew I was expected.

"Prince Kanemi is inside," he intoned, taking over the reins of my horse. "He has been asking about you. You are Mallam Ilia, I suppose?"

Wondering how he knew my name, I bowed and went in. The whole place was in darkness, except for the little spot of light beneath which Zarah sat. I had walked barely a few feet in that direction when strong hands gripped me and guided me towards her. Then the lights were brought, and I saw that I was surrounded by about a dozen youths, all in cloaks and turbans. The scabbards dangling from their hips told me of dangerous work to follow.

Prince Kanemi appeared, dressed in a rich, velvet turban embroidered with gold. From his shoulders hung a gay cloak, gathered about the middle with a large piece of jewellery. He waved his gold-crowned staff and the music stopped.

"Welcome, my sons," he said. "Tonight, one of you is going to win the hand of my daughter Zarah. But he must be the bravest of you all. We live in times when a man's might is his right." He paused suddenly and looked at me. "You have all heard of the game called *Shanchi*, I presume?"

We were silent, and he went on:

"It is not a game for faint hearts. But he who thinks that Zarah is not a sufficient prize to induce him to take part, let him leave now."

Nobody moved, and Kanemi's face darkened.

"Some of you here will not breathe tomorrow's air. For this night *shanchi* may claim you." He walked down a number of steps, inviting us to follow him. Kanemi led us to an open field, in the middle of which was a ring. "This is where the game will be played. You are all to go in there. The lights will be put out. In the darkness you will try to get your man. Do what you can to disable him. At the end of the game, the man who is left becomes Zarah's husband."

"Your Majesty," said a thick-set man. "How do we 'disable' our man?"

"You have swords, haven't you?"

"Yes," said the man. "I—I was thinking . . ." He stared about him timidly, the sweat standing on his face. "I was thinking—if the man died..."

"If he dies, we remove him."

Kanemi turned to us. "Make ready, men." He waved his staff, and the air was at once filled with the blare of trumpets. When the harsh notes ceased, Kanemi said something to Zarah, and she gave us her own brand of music. Bringing out her *gwoje*—an instrument rather like a violin—she played so sweetly and so softly that the night stood still and listened to her. I could not help feeling that there was something mournful about her music, and that great sorrow would be the outcome of this contest.

"To the ring!" shouted Kanemi.

We crowded in. The enclosure was small and as soon as we were inside, the lights were put out. I stood clutching the ropes for a moment, too blinded to see the dim shapes of my rivals, even though they were within a few yards of me. At that moment, a strange fear came over me. I realized suddenly that death might be my portion in this game; that I might not win the hand I coveted so much. I had heard of *shanchi* before Kanemi explained it to us, but never before had I imagined that I should play it, and for such high stakes.

In a way, I am glad the British came to Kano so soon after and stamped out such dreadful customs. But the year I speak about was 1902, and human life at that time was worth about as much as a fowls.

Just as I had become used to the darkness, a man stole past me, creeping so that I might not hear his footsteps. I drew my knife, crouched and sprang like a leopard upon him. He groaned and leapt backwards; a second later, a piercing scream told its own story; someone had finished him off. The lights were brought in; Kanemi's men came into the ring and carried the bleeding body out of the ring. During that interval, men studied the positions of their opponents.

Again, we were all in darkness. Two simultaneous groans filled the air. In came the lights to the ring and two bodies were carried out. The game of *shanchi* was warming up. Three men gone: nine left. Every time the ring was lighted, Kanemi smacked his lips with satisfaction, and smoothed his waxy moustaches. Zarah, I noticed, had stopped playing her *gwoje*, and, sitting up on her sofa, was staring wide-eyed at the ring. She looked truly lovely. The fire in her eye made me wish I could win her, and I determined to fight to the death.

One by one, we thinned out. At last. Only four of us were left. Of the eight who had been removed, four were quite disabled and four were quite dead. Excitement mounted among the spectators as the four of us stood in the light of the lamps, panting and glaring.

When the lights went out, I threw myself down on my stomach, and, with a sudden spin, gripped someone by the legs and threw him down. He stabbed furiously at me, but I was on top of him like a cat. Two quick stabs, and he was silent. The body of my first victim was removed from the ring.

Three men left. For a brief moment I saw my two adversaries. They were big men. One of them stood well over six feet in height. He was looking at me, and I knew that he would make for me the moment he lights went out again. And so, it happened. He swept past me just as I sprang aside. There was a wild yell of "Yee—whoo!"

Regaining my balance, I leapt in his direction, striking out with a short knife drawn from the band around my elbow. I must have hit him in a vital spot, for he fell without a sound. When the lights went up, I gasped with disappointment. The man who had fallen was not the bigger man, but my second adversary. He had rushed at me in the same instant and had caught the thrust.

There were now only two of us left. My opponent indeed was an enormous man, big-jawed and long-toothed.

"You're going to die now," he growled. "Your knife can do nothing to me. I have swallowed the medicine against steel."

He jabbed himself suddenly with his own knife, and the blade bent. He threw it down and drew another from his wrist. The lights were removed, and I was alone with him. I have never been nearer death in my life. What chance had I against him? He could smash me with his fist; and my knife, my sole aid, was useless.

I was feeling stiff and sore, and the prospect of being stabbed made me nervous and breathless. I didn't know how to last it out. Would a miracle happen? Would Kanemi call it all off and say he had changed his mind?

For a long time, we manoeuvred around the ring.

I moved slowly with the quietness and caution of a chameleon, pausing to listen for him. But never once did I hear him. We met suddenly, and he stabbed furiously at me. His elbow, catching me on the head, sent a shiver down my spine. With that sudden strength born of panic, I made a wild upthrust at his body, but the knife bent like a pin, and I knew then what he had meant when he said that he swallowed a medicine against steel. He was wearing a coat of chain-armour.

That realization summarized my chances. Henceforth, cunning rather than valour would be my weapon. He gave chase as I ran. I had no clear idea in my head what to do when my breath failed me. I ran zigzag round the ring.

Then my luck turned. All of a sudden, he fell. I was quick to see what happened. He had stepped on the knife which he himself had thrown down, and the bent razor-edged blade had pierced his bare food as easily as the sun pierces the clouds.

I saw that now was my chance. Drawing my knife, I thrust it at his bare neck. He was powerless. Given the same opportunity, I am quite certain that he would have killed me. But I merely disabled him, and therein lay my mistake: a mistake which I have regretted all my life.

I left him lying there in his own blood, while Kanemi took me to my prize.

"Zarah," he said. "You have won a brave husband.

"A lucky one," I corrected.

When all the excitement of the contest had died down, arrangements were made for Zarah and me to leave for home. Her father detailed a number of horsemen to accompany us, and later a company of women brought Zarah's things. From what I gathered of their talk, none of them appeared particularly happy about my victory. Zarah, they hinted, was a woman who carried bad luck with her, and her beauty they feared would bring me ruin and unhappiness, as it had done to others.

I was not happy to hear all this, but I quickly tried to put their warnings out of my mind.

DEATH BY THE SWORD

Zarah proved herself a most capable wife and, for the first year, we were very happy. She was not too proud to do a certain amount of housework, and in the evenings when we went out for a canter, she carried herself like the true princess she was, and I was proud of her.

But, withal, I sometimes caught her falling into pensive moods, and for days on end she would speak to no one, not even to me. The first time she behaved in this way I was most worried, but as time went on, I grew to regard these moods as part of that complex nature of a woman which makes her difficult to understand.

The story of Zarah came to me in little snatches: from conversations I overheard, from open talk that went on in the town when I was around, and from gossip tactlessly flung into my ears.

It appears that she was the second daughter of Kanemi, Prince of the Tuaregs. Kanemi loved her best of all his daughters and betrothed her at an early age to another Tuareg Prince whom she grew up to hate. On the night when the horses came to take her to her husband, Zarah disappeared. She was found some weeks later taking refuge in the house of one of her former woman servants.

Kanemi was very angry about this, since the marriage, now no longer possible, would have increased his political influence. For many days he thought hard how best to punish her. As a man who loved fighting, nothing appealed to his imagination more than gambling her away at a game of *shanchi*. On the night of his decision, he rode round the town, inviting young men to the contest.

Of those others whom Zarah had ruined, I did not hear much; nor did I find out anything definite about her beauty being dangerous. Perhaps I was worrying myself unnecessarily and it had been idle gossip. But it came to my ears in whispers that just before I won her, Zarah had developed a great love for a man called Mallam Usuman. This man, who posed as the son of an Emir, was wealthy and influential, and fonder of the sword than he was of work. My friends who knew him well advised me to leave the town before he became well again.

"Is he sick, then?" I asked.

"Yes. He was wounded on the night of the *shanchi*."

"Wait: what did he look like?"

The description I heard was rather vague, but it

led me to suspect that Mallam Usuman was no other than my last adversary in the ring: the man who boasted that he had "swallowed the medicine against steel". But I couldn't be sure just then.

I was in my room one evening listening to Zarah's *gwoje*, when someone shouted greetings at the door, and I came out. It was Mallam Usuman, and behind him were three mounted men. Their very bearing spelt trouble, as their horses stamped impatiently. Usuman appeared rather pale by daylight, and a deep knife-slash marked his neck and cheek.

"Ho, Ilia," he roared. "Look at this!"

He put down a bundle from his horse and invited me to examine it. It was the mutilated body of a child. It must have died some time earlier.

"What is the meaning of this?" I asked. "How did he die?"

Usuman exploded: "How did he die? My men, do you hear a question? How did he die?"

"Have I offended by asking?"

"He's playing innocent," Usuman told them.

I did not follow what he meant. "What have you come to say?" I snapped.

"Ilia," said Usuman. "You killed this boy, and we have come to take you before the law."

If he had shot at me with his gun, I could not have been more surprised. "Killed him?" I gasped.

"Yes. What else can it be? When a man leaves his horse to run wild all over the town…"

"My horse?"

"Show it to him."

He made an impatient movement, and a horse was brought before me. It was Wutsia, my favourite horse. Its forelegs were stained with blood.

"Is that not your horse?" he asked.

I admitted that it was.

"This morning your horse ran through the town, riderless. This boy was on the roadway. Your horse knocked him down and killed him. You ought to take more care of your livestock, Ilia." He turned to the men and said sharply: "Take him along!"

They took me and put me in prison. It was unfair, of course. I knew nothing about the whole affair. There was no means of verifying their story, no assurance that I should be given a hearing. They merely threw me into jail and walked away. My cell was a little room, airless, and shared by twenty to thirty other men. The season was at its hottest in Kano, and smallpox ravaged the town. Every day a few men died in our cell, only to be replaced by as many. The jailers were sometimes too busy to remove the corpses, and then we had dead men for company: not a very happy situation, I assure you.

While I was in prison, important events were happening in the outside world. It was the year 1903, the year of the Kano rising. You may remember what caused the rising. The Emir of Keffi and the Magaji of Zaria had come to take refuge at Kano because they were badly "wanted" by the British. The story went that the British had sent one of their representatives to interview these great rulers; but instead of giving him audience the servants of the rulers had seized the white man and murdered him. That was the accepted story. But we in the prison knew that the murderer was none other than Mallam Usuman.

Early one morning, we heard the thunder of big guns, the crash of shells, and the shouts of the inhabitants. There was panic everywhere, even among us, and our jailers were nowhere to be seen. Neglected and without food, we heard no explanation of what was happening until later in the afternoon, when a handful of African riflemen came into the prison yard, broke open our barricades, and set us free.

When I came out, my limbs were stiff, and I was weak. I was so exhausted that I was compelled to lie down on the ground until one of the African troops gave me something to drink. Gradually I regained my strength; my head no longer swam, and my feet trod fairly steadily when I left the prison yard.

My first thought was my home. Would Sarah still be there? As I walked, I noticed that the town was much altered. There were broken bottles on the walls, piles of thorn bushes blockaded the roads, the ditches were deeper, and everybody I met carried a weapon of some sort. One of the houses near my own must have been badly damaged, for the roof was gone, and part of the wall had fallen in. My fears became suddenly overpowering. Was Zarah dead? Did she lie beneath a heap of earth, her delicate body mangled by some cruel weight?

I got to the house in a state of the wildest excitement. The door had fallen in, and I had to scale some splintered wood debris. The goats were running here and there, and the servants had all left except one who followed me bewildered from one room to another, saying nothing, offering no help, but merely getting in my way.

As I came to each room, I called:

"Zarah!"

No answer. I listened but heard nothing save the dismal moaning of the wind.

"Zarah! . . ."

Still no answer: only that terrible wind.

I made for our private room.

"Zarah! . . ."

Then I heard a strange sound. It sounded like the cry of someone in great pain, a person to whom immediate help would mean everything. I burst into the room. Just then a man turned and drew his sword. There behind lay my Zarah, petrified with fear and well-nigh fainting. The man was glowering at me, his sword drawn. One glance at those dark eyebrows and I recognized him—Usuman, the thief, cheat, highway robber, murderer—the man who had put me in prison out of envy. I was almost mad with rage. With scarcely a thought for my own safety, and forgetting that I was entirely unarmed, I sprang at him. He made a desperate thrust, which I just escaped as I stumbled on a fallen brick.

He was well and strong, while I was weak from the starving, carried out under his orders. My efforts were feeble. I knew for certain that my recklessness would have cost me my life, had not Zarah staggered to her feet, and, seizing a club, brought it down with all her strength on his head.

The big Usuman sank to his knees, and we both thought he had been killed. I embraced Zarah, and we talked hurriedly of what had been happening in my absence. She told me how Usuman had been tormenting her ever since I had left the house.

"Ilia is going to rot away in prison," he had told her. "He'll never come out of that hole. Follow me, Zarah. I'll make you a wealthy woman—the wife of a future Emir."

She had always refused his temptings, and on many occasions had told her retainers not to let him in. He had kept away for short periods—presumably when on some murderous errand—but during the Kano rising she suddenly found him in her rooms, telling her that the city had surrendered, that I was dead, and that the most reasonable thing for her to do was to follow him and leave the city before the British came. They were still arguing about this when I had entered the house.

I looked at Usuman where he lay senseless among the wreckage. "Do you know, Zarah, that there is a price on this man's head? He is accused of killing an English captain at Keffi: that must have been the reason why he was so anxious to leave the town. As a matter of fact, the British forces have occupied the town, but there is no fighting going on: we can still live here if we choose..."

"What shall we do?" asked Zarah.

"Are you prepared to follow me?"

As we spoke, the fallen Usuman groaned. I went over and picked up his sword. Zarah was behind me as I began to sort out my valuables: my Koran, my chaplet, my talismans.

She had little to pack: her jewels and gold and other feminine ornaments went into a little black box which she had brought with her from her father's house.

"Is that all?" I asked her.

"Yes," she smiled.

"Then I must saddle the horses. We may have to ride all night. Get something we can eat on the way. I'm very hungry."

There was only one of my horses left: a black beast, long-legged, big-chested and full of stamina. I saddled her and turned to Zarah.

Then I noticed that Mallam Usuman had risen and was now staggering towards her. He was a thing of terror. His hair was shaggy, his arms swayed menacingly, his teeth here bared. In one or two strides, he was beside the terrified Zarah, and had gripped her.

"You shall not take her with you," he roared, clasping her tightly to himself.

"I shall!"

"You shan't!" He drew a small knife, and, still holding Zarah close to him, invited me to face him.

How could I? Sword in hand, I stood for a moment confused, while his fiery eyes mocked me. Then Zarah kicked and bit at him, and his hold was slackened. He was struggling to regain his hold of her when I made a clean thrust at his ribs. But villain that he was, little did I suspect his trap. At precisely the moment when I lunged at him, Usuman in a flash clutched Zarah and held her as a shield before his own body. The accident happened before I could check myself.

She fell right in line with the sword point, and the weapon ran straight through her heart. Usuman flung her aside, and his laughter still rings in my ears to this day. As he ran towards the door, he roared with laughter:

"What did I tell you? Ha, ha, ha! I said you wouldn't take her."

"Ibrahim!... Ibrahim, come back."

It was Zarah's voice. I had already bounded over the fallen body and was catching up with Usuman when I heard it. I went back at once. Zarah was breathing her last. She had lost a lot of blood and her eyes were pale. She gasped and panted when she tried to speak, and her words were inaudible. Beautiful Zarah! Beautiful even in death! Kneeling beside her, I could not bring myself to believe that this was true: that she was leaving me forever.

"Zarah! . . ."

She turned her eyes towards me.

"Zarah; can you hear me now? I shall not rest, for I shall know no peace until I have avenged you."

She was still trying to form some words. Her eyes were closed, her lips pale.

"Ib—ra—h..."

She died, with my uncompleted name on her lips.

It was some time later, as I still sat beside her body, that the servant made a remark which broke through my stupor.

"Our mistress is dead," she said. "She was so brave while you were away and prayed for your return."

I looked up. The words chased each other round my brain. Consciousness came back to me, and with it, a sense of purpose. What was I doing here, kneeling beside the body of a dead woman?

I turned to the servant. "Here is some money," I said. "Call the others and see that you mistress receives a burial fit for the wife of Mallam Alhaji Ibrahim Ilia. I go on my mission."

With her package of jewels and gold under my arm, and murder in my eyes, I rode into the gathering dusk.

USUMAN, TERROR OF THE NORTH

As you will hear, it was some time before I set eyes on Mallam Usuman again. After I left my house, I rode round the town hoping to find Yisa, my trading agent, but he was nowhere to be seen. There was no knowing whether he had been killed in the skirmish or had fled with my merchandise and money. I had therefore to pursue Usuman with neither food nor funds.

About two weeks after the death of Zarah, I received news that Mallam Usuman and his supporters had assembled a large force and were even making their way down from Sokoto to Kano.

The British force at Kano was not very large. There were a number of officers and trained Africans, but many had been killed during the Kano campaign. And so, when they appealed for help, I quickly volunteered, though for no other reason than to meet Usuman face to face on the battlefield.

We were about a thousand strong. In the early hours of the morning, we left Kano and moved out to meet them. Some time in the afternoon, we sighted them. The scorching sun shone upon weapons of all sorts. Horses reared and capered, kicking up dust, while the men on foot brandished spears, and bows and arrows. They paused when they sighted us and held a brief consultation.

Our General gave a sharp order, and at once the soldiers formed themselves into a square. We were given whispered commands to hold our fire until they were within eighty yards of us. How well I remember it. I have never seen a braver fight. There they were—an army at least ten times our number— charging down on us and yelling like devils, their turbans flying, their gowns billowing, their horses groaning and panting; and there we were, crouching in the sun, waiting as quietly as if the men were paying us a friendly visit.

As they came within range, the General's arm came down sharply, and we let them have it. They were shocked; many of them dropped dead, and the rest stopped, then retreated. Out of range, they reformed their troops, and again attacked, only to suffer even greater losses. It began to look as if Usuman and his friends would never get back the city. The air was thick with dust, the field was littered with the bodies of the dead, the vultures were already hovering overhead; and yet there we lay on our stomachs, hoping and praying that this tremendous horde of men would not overrun us, now that our ammunition was getting low. In fact, this was what I prayed for: that the fighting would become a hand-to-hand affair, so that I might meet Usuman.

Just at the moment when we heard the order to fix bayonets, Usuman's men turned and fled. And then we saw the reason: another British force had cut them off from the rear, offering them no alternative. A very disappointing end for me.

When I eventually got back to Kano, no one could tell me the whereabouts of Mallam Usuman. Many people said that they had seen him at Sokoto, and some reported that after that last onslaught he was seen at the head of the retreating troops.

I remained in the British army for a little while. It seemed the only thing to do. But I soon became restless and anxious to fulfil my promise to myself and to Zarah. Every time I thought of her as she had lain dying from the sword thrust in that wrecked house, my conscience pricked me, and I realized that my great mission in life was yet to be done.

At that time, the whole of Northern Nigeria was in disorder. Some Emirs had fled; some they say were later arrested and punished. No one was very sure at this transitional period who was really ruling us. The white men were still studying conditions, and in any case were too few to do anything definite.

The roads at this time were about as safe as a lion's den. You could not travel outside Kano without being waylaid by masked horsemen and killed or robbed. One of the wildest and most notorious groups at large was said to be headed by my enemy Malam Usuman. He had terrorized the whole of Northern Nigeria from Maiduguri in the east to Sokoto in the west.

The news held that he was to be seen in a group with four other Mallams of repute, under pretext of going on a pilgrimage; that he had passed safely through English territory—but that, safely through, he resorted once again to cheating, plundering and killing.

I longed for the day when we should again stand face to face, with swords in our hands and fire in our eyes.

2
USUMAN IS AT LARGE

THE INDIAN WOMAN

For several years after the Kano rising, Usuman was at large. He and his gang continued plundering and looting until the very name "Usuman" came to mean terror—a name that was mentioned only in whispers by men, while mothers saved their crying children a tear or two by calling "Usuman! Here he comes…"

The British still "wanted" him for the murder of the English captain whom they had sent to interview the Emir of Keffi, and I "wanted" him for wilfully causing the death of my Zarah.

It was a Hausa soldier who first saw him in hiding. Mallam Usuman had camped for the night at the foot of a hill. In the evening, he was sitting beside his tent, saying his prayers, when suddenly a sharp prod in the middle of his back caused him to turn round. A man with a rifle stood over him.

"Usuman, you are my prisoner."

If Usuman was afraid, he did not show it. He was alone in the camp. His partners had gone out on a raid and would not be back till midnight. Usuman knew this; he also knew how helpless he was, with his own rifle inside the tent; so, he decided to play for time.

Seeing that this captor was a fellow tribesman, he spoke to him familiarly: "Mallam, I am indeed your prisoner. But why? You are a true Muslim. Why must you betray your own brother to unbelievers?"

The soldier frowned.

"I am a soldier," he said. "And my duty comes first."

"Truly, your duty comes first. But how would you like to join forces with Usuman, terror of the North, and make money in plenty, and live in luxury? People in my army do not eat dry, black bread."

"They warned me about this," the soldier said. "They told me you would want to buy me."

Usuman's tone became suddenly confidential.

"Listen, my friend: if you really want prisoners, I'll tell you something. The others will soon be back, and then you can take the whole lot of us. As a matter of fact, I'm getting tired of this life…"

"My time is short," said the soldier.

As he spoke, a number of men appeared. Usuman gasped with surprise when he realized that they were not his men. The new arrivals carried rifles and haversacks and were clearly members of the British army. They took Mallam Usuman away from the camp, and struck out for Kano, moving as fast as they could.

They did not get far. About a mile or two from the camp they fell into an ambush. From both sides of the road came a wild howl, then a sudden rush like an overwhelming gale, and, before they realized what the position was, the soldiers were down on their faces, senseless. That great rogue quietly removed their ammunition and their rifles, remarking before he left the scene:

"You didn't want to join me; now you've got your reward."

But the incident had taught him a lesson, and henceforth Usuman went about with three of his best men, and all were heavily armed.

It was still in the early nineteen hundreds, and the popular means of transporting loads in the North was by head. White men moved about in hammocks, winding their way through the bush, and cursing the mosquitoes. Usuman knew this well, and soon after his encounter with the soldiers he had somehow gleaned the information that an important British official was on his way to Kano, carrying money and food for the white men.

Usuman held consultation with his men.

"We are in great need of money," he told them, as they sat beneath the trees, their eyes peering out across the open country. "But we are badly armed. Apart from the four rifles, our knives and fists, we have nothing. And they will be protected by a large number of machine-guns, rifles, bayonets and those little things that burst and blow-up rocks."

They decided that surprise would be their chief

weapon and, placing a scout on top of a tree, they made ready. About half an hour later the scout shouted down:

"Usuman! I see a cloud of dust…"

Usuman sprang to his feet, and asked: "Are there many people?"

"Hundreds!"

"What shall we do?" asked the others.

"Do?" said Usuman scornfully. "He who is afraid may leave now, before it is too late."

Those three men had too often seen what happened to others who obeyed this invitation to be tempted to throw away their lives so easily. For it went without saying that if any one of them had dared to leave, Usuman would have shot him in the back.

"Make for the money boxes," Usuman resumed, when the silence remained unbroken.

They climbed into the trees and waited. Usuman could now see the long column, winding its way across the tree-dotted stretch before them. He cocked his rifle and held it at the ready.

As they came nearer, he could make out that, contrary to what he expected, there were three white men, and well protected they were by a ring of soldiers armed to the teeth. A few yards from the tree the procession stopped, and for one tense moment even the dauntless Usuman gulped with fear as he thought they had seen him. But the white men were merely stretching their legs and admiring the scenery.

"Listen!" whispered Usuman. "I think the money is in those black boxes. Go for them at once; we'll meet behind the rocks."

Usuman winked at the men, and together they got down and raced for the carriers bearing the strongboxes. A short and swift engagement followed. No shots were fired. The raiders were in the midst of the team one moment, and, next moment, they had knocked down the strong-box, Usuman had dismounted a man and got into the saddle himself, and as he reared the horse round the moneybox was handed to him, and he rode away amidst a cloud of dust.

It was a dodge they had rehearsed many times before, and Usuman rode off with the conviction that the others would soon join him at the appointed spot.

He brought his horse to a standstill near a stream flowing between tall rocks, and, leaving it to feed on the tender grass nearby, took the box and forced it open with his rifle. He was shocked. Though it had looked like a strong box, there was nothing in it but cartridges and handcuffs.

Usuman flung the box into the river, muttering:

"What am I going to do with old iron?"

After waiting there for the rest of the night, Usuman decided that harm must have come to his friends, and he went to sleep. Next day, he set out, hungrier than before, and even more desperate. There was no knowing when the next transport would come through. He had missed a golden chance. Such information was none too easily come by.

For months on end, he roamed wild—alone and unsupported—with no company save the stolen horse. He was watering his horse one afternoon, when above the lapping of the stream, he thought he heard the noise of grinding wheels. The noise grew louder, and, turning round, he saw, rising skywards, a billowing cloud of dust. This was the chance he had been waiting for.

Walking cautiously up the bank, he saw a bullock team grinding its way northwards. By his reckoning, about five passengers sat inside the coach, and they were travelling with the ease and comfort of those who suspect no misfortune. The thickset driver swished his whip carelessly at the bulls.

Mallam Usuman quickly guided his horse up the bank of the stream, and, riding slowly along, studied the transport for a time. Experience told him that they had been travelling for some time and were therefore very tired. He dug his heels into the flanks of his horse. In a moment, he had drawn up beside them and levelled his gun.

"Whoever you are," he snarled, "you can choose."

The transport stopped, and the river turned his sun-scorched face towards him. There was anger in his flaming eyes.

"Which do you choose," Usuman went on, "your life or your money?"

"There—there is no money," stammered the driver.

"Don't lie!"

Usuman, with his quick eye, had already seen the

wooden box beneath the driver's seat; but now, as the passengers began to complain and show signs of terror, Usuman noticed that there was a woman in the carriage. She was sitting tightly wedged in between the other passengers, calm and cool. She lifted her black veil for a moment and Usuman's eyes widened at the sight of her face. She was beautiful.

The driver must have been watching him, for he said in Hausa: "You like her then? Unfortunately, she is not for you . . ."

"You rat!" snapped Usuman. "Throw down the money and drive on."

The driver glanced from the bore of the rifle into Usuman's face and obeyed. He got down, fumbled for a moment, and was bringing out something from under the box when Usuman shot him in the hand and a British revolver dropped to the ground.

"Now, will you put down the box?"

Cursing, the driver pushed down the box with his left hand and climbed back into his seat.

"Not yet," said Usuman. He turned and winked at the lady. "Open the carriage and let her step down!"

The driver's jaw dropped.

"Mallam, I swear she's the wife of an Arab Prince. I—I've been commissioned to take her back to her husband."

Like something pre-arranged, all the passengers suddenly let out a howl: "Yee-whoo! . . . Wai-O!"

The driver leapt back into his seat and waved his arms frantically. From the distance a number of horsemen were charging towards them. Usuman saw the danger in which he stood and made up his mind quickly.

He leapt down from his horse and struck the driver on the head. With his left hand, he tore open the door of the carriage, brandishing his rifle. In the distance, the gowns of his enemies floated in the wind as they galloped towards him, shouting as they came. They were now so near that he might have made out their faces, but for the dust. He dealt the beautiful woman a blow with his open fist and she fell senseless across the door. Then he lifted her body into the saddle. There was no time to pick up the money.

When the horsemen came near, he had disappeared. They dispersed in various directions, but no trace of Usuman was to be found.

Usuman rode far into the night until he met a nomadic herdsman who gave him shelter. The robber had told him that he was from Kano, driven out of his home by the British, that the woman was his wife and that he was now without any worldly goods.

Usuman must have lived with that cattleman for quite a year before I met him. I was going to Sokoto at the time, and my way took me by the cattleman's hut, where I stopped for refreshment. His wife was very kind to me.

"We have so little mild these days," she apologized. "The soldier and his wife take everything we have, pay nothing for it and, when we complain, he threatens to shoot us."

"You have a soldier staying with you?"

"Yes. He is from the Kano wars."

"What is he like?"

"Oh! A very big man and his wife" —she closed her eyes— "very nice!"

"I am from the Kao wars myself; I want to see this man."

At that the woman grew panicky. "He does not want to see anybody. His temper is very bad—"

I got down from my horse and went towards the hut. As a man who knew the country at the time, it was natural that I should be cautious. I had my rifle in my hands; my eyes and ears missed nothing that might be dangerous.

The door of the hut was open when I came to it. Inside the hut I saw Usuman and the woman too. She was a beautiful creature, but somehow, she did not look Nigerian. Mallam Usuman himself had grown considerably thinner and more unkempt, and his eyes glowered at me from the semi-darkness. They very sight of him brought back all the loathing I had for the scoundrel. Controlling my voice, I said:

"We've met, Usuman!" My hands were trembling. "Come out and let us settle it."

From where I stood, I could easily have shot him, but that would have been a cowardly act. It was not like me to take advantage of a weak enemy. I could see that he was looking with anxiety at his rifle which lay just out of his reach, behind his wife. He said nothing, and again I invited him.

"Did you hear me, Usuman? Come out before I murder you!"

There was a brief pause; then Usuman moved suddenly. The door of the hut shut, sending up a cloud of dust. A rifle cracked, and a bullet whistled past my ear. I fired back. A woman screamed. The hut—a mere grass affair—burst open at the back, Mallam Usuman emerged, mounted his horse, and rode off.

It had all happened within a moment. I saw the dust raised by his horse as he galloped away. When it cleared, he was out of sight, and all was quiet as death. Just then the silence was broken by the wail of a tiny child.

I picked up the child. He was strikingly like Usuman. He had the same piercing eyes, the same savage set of the lips. It was easy for me to hate this child and to want to destroy it. But after all, I reasoned, why visit the sins of the father on the son? My score would be settled with Mallam Usuman, and no other.

"There now," I said, gathering him up in the cloth in which he lay. "Don't cry . . . come now, let's take you to Kano. There we're sure to find friends to bring you up. You father's my enemy, but I shall pay for your upbringing. Allah sees!"

I can assure you; I did not enjoy carrying out my decision. The roads were dangerous, and the child was not the ideal travelling companion for a man leading a precarious life. But finally, I settled Usuman's son among friends at Kano, and came away.

About two years later, something happened in Northern Nigeria which disturbed the peace of every normal man. It was the year 1906. A man called Satiru had come into prominence and had given out that he was a *Mahdi*—a kind of heaven—sent religious leader.

I was staying at Sokoto during the following year. I had already put young Usuman, for whom I felt a responsibility, under a guardian, a Mallam of some repute and standing, when I began to make investigations into the Satiru movement. I found one thing of imprtance: the Sultan was by no means enthusiastic about it; I also learned that Satiru had joined forces with my old enemy Usuman and that they were at that moment preparing an army to march against the British.

The Sultan sent a messenger to Satiru.

"Tell him to come here. In the name of the Prophet, tell him to come. Tell him that I, the spiritual head of all Muslims, want to speak to him."

The messenger rode off at dawn.

He never returned. And no one knows to this day what actually happened to him.

Desperation drove the Sultan to appeal to the British Resident.

"This is the position," he explained. "Satiru is a mere pretender. He is no religious leader. I have sent a message to him, but he won't come, and he won't return my messenger."

"Well?" said the Resident.

"I want permission to send an army against him."

The white man smiled quietly.

"My friend," he said, "you have done well. But remember, this is not your war: it is our war."

I rejoined the British army, with great hopes of meeting Usuman of the field of battle. We set out for the village of Satiru on a Thursday morning. That day we marched until it was dusk, stopping only at Bodinga, where we slept. Bodinga was a village some few miles from Satiru. Next morning, at about eleven-thirty, we were again on our way. There were about three companies of us, some horsemen but mainly infantry.

We stopped just outside the village. Those who were not fighting men—people like myself—were sent to collect fodder for the horses. We set off, accompanied by seven soldiers and one sergeant for protection. The rest of the company began to take up position. Some went off to fine tree-butts, rocks, and such things that might be used for building a low wall. Our commander immediately sent a messenger on horseback into the village.

Hours dragged by. We had dug ourselves in, we had eaten a hearty meal, and were waiting for action. All eyes were turned in the direction of the village. Then a horse ran riderless towards us, while behind it on the wall of the village a man was waving something black.

"The messenger's horse!" somebody gasped.

"But where is the messenger himself?"

The white men, who had been looking through their glasses, answered the question. They told us that the man who was standing on the wall of the village was waving nothing but a human head. He was a big man with a wild beard, and a cut in his cheek.

My blood boiled when I heard that.

"That is Usuman!" I shouted.

"Who is Usuman?"

"A wild creature; a man who claims to be the son of the Emir."

"We don't know him. The Emir has no such son."

Our officers warned us that they could see Satiru making preparations for action. Dane guns, hatchets, and clubs were being distributed, and the inhabitants were rushing hither and thither in an excited state.

At the command, those who had already formed a square began to move forward. Just then when our troops were still manoeuvring to get into position, Satiru came down upon us, yelling and shooting. Three Englishmen were killed, and our troops had to retreat in considerable disorder.

Satiru had defeated us in that first encounter. After we had retired, he had captured one of the Englishmen, and had tried to get information out of him about how to work the field guns. Threats, torture and bullying were alike to no avail. Somewhat out of temper, Satiru shot him.

Our broken troops got back to Sokoto, disgraced by an untrained fanatic. We had no courage to go back just then against such numbers as the *Mahdi* had, and so we appealed to Zungeru for help. That was several hundred miles away; there were no roads as we know them today, no telegraph lines, and robbers roamed wild. It took the best part of two months before our messengers got there and came back with the cheerful news that help was forthcoming soon. Meantime, there was every possibility that Satiru would swoop down upon us and exterminate us before that happy event took place.

But the help did come; and during out interval of anxiety, Satiru did nothing about his own position. That Saturday morning when we left Sokoto for the second encounter, he was probably no more aware of his own danger than of the fact that heaven had not sent him to lead his own people. This time, we knew what we were up against. The moment we came within sight of the village, we opened fire. Satiru, surprised out of his spiritual meditations, had scarcely time to get ready.

Within a few moments of our arrival, the place was a mass of flames and smoke. Goats and sheep ran here and there, panic-stricken. The people themselves poured out of their houses, yelling and trying to save their property.

Satiru was captured and made prisoner. He was a much younger man than I had expected. His long lean face belied that fire which burned in his heart and drew followers to him by the thousand.

I was making a final tour of the village of Satiru, my eyes wide open, my ears tuned to hear the least suspicious noise. I knew what I was looking for. It was evening then, and the sun had gone down. I remember that day well: not very warm and there was dust and smoke about. Suddenly I came upon a very conspicuous building. It had a flag on top—a sign that it was a drinking-house. The roof had fallen in, table which suggested quite recent use.

I looked round: there was no one in sight. I had come to the conclusion that the room was empty and had turned my back when—from nowhere—came a heavy blow on the back of my head. My left arm felt suddenly numb, and I went down.

Voices came to me as in a dream.

"Wai. . .!" said a woman. "You've killed him."

"Yes," said a man. "Let's go."

It was Usuman's voice.

THE SCHOOL AT MECCA

I was a cripple after that. My left arm was useless, dead. I found that it would be futile for me to continue a life of adventure. I had learnt a lesson, and now it was time to devote myself to less exciting pursuits—to things that belong to the soul.

After the Satiru rebellion, I apprenticed myself to Mallam Gobir, a man well read in the Koran, and indeed a scholar. He improved my mind and taught me great truths that made life more purposeful, and more worthwhile. It must have been about 1910 that we set out on a pilgrimage to Mecca, travelling on camels across the Great Desert. We took plenty of time over the journey, for my teacher was an old man, and he prided himself on his understanding of the desert and its mysteries.

We met a lot of other scholars at Mecca, and my tutor was never so pleased as when he saw cultured men who put into practice the very things he had been trying to impart to me: people who loved their fellow-men, said their prayers morning, noon, and night, had no fear of death, and never worried themselves unduly over their grave misfortunes, but hoped that by Allah's grace it would all come right in the end. I could see peace on their calm faces: an inward peace which made me feel that I had been a fool ever to think of killing Usuman because he had caused the death of my Zarah.

But Mallam Gobir was destined not to return with me. He became ill shortly after we got to Mecca, and, within a week, died. It must have been the cold of the desert mornings that did it. I remember that he complained many times about a weakness in his chest.

Before he died, he called me to his side and spoke to me.

"Promise me, Ilia, my son. Promise me one thing."
"Yes, my master."

"Promise me that you will always live according to the Prophet, that you will do all you can to be good, to propagate the faith. . ."

My heart glowed with warmth. "I promise," I whispered.

"That's all I ask."

A smile crossed his face. It was such a grand old face, compassionate and gentle: not like mine which has been hardened by the desire for vengeance. That smile was still on his face when he breathed his last.

I rose up and covered his dead face with a white sheet. As I made my way to the place of prayer, my heart suddenly stood still. What irony of Fate after my promise to my late teacher to come face to face with the very man I hated most in the world! He was washing his feet near the big red pots, and when he saw me, his eyes widened with surprise. Seconds seemed like hours. I stood as if paralysed. When he had finished, he stood up, took water into his mouth, rinsed it, and spat it straight into my face. I reminded myself that I was going to keep my promise to the old teacher; so, I let that go. But Usuman was looking for trouble. Throughout prayer-time, he made himself as distracting and annoying as he could, and when prayers were over, and the more serious Mallams sat cross-legged meditating, Usuman came over to me and whispered:

"So you didn't die!"

I did not answer but continued with my devotions. He placed his mouth to my ear and said, "What about the Indian Woman?"

I turned a surprised face to him, and he added: "The mother of my son."

I tried to ignore Usuman, but he was so overpowering that, although I was occupied counting my chaplet, my mind was restless. Here was Usuman at Mecca, probably making atonement for his misdeeds, and in the midst of it being not only unpleasant to a fellow sinner but also completely callous about the way he had treated "the Indian woman", and also about the fate of his son. But I had decided to give up all hate and ignore him. After Usuman had tried in vain to provoke me, he gathered up the folds of his gown and laughed.

"I see why you're so quiet, Ilia. Your arm is dead. You can fight no more."

"Where shall we meet?" I asked hotly.

"You know the river by the large mosque?"

"No; but I'll find it."

"There are three date palms leading down to that river. Wait for me at the third. There will be a moon, so we won't need a light to bury your body."

He laughed, winked at me, then mingled with the other Mallams.

I was wild with fury. How could I—a small enough man to start with—face Usuman, the giant, with my paralysed arm and no hope to win? But I had impetuously given him my word and would certainly meet him bravely. It had been whole; I had never once had an opportunity to meet him in such a duel as this.

As he said, there was plenty of moon. I had no difficulty in finding the place but, when I arrived, Usuman was nowhere to be seen. I stood leaning against the palm and gazing at the river as it caught the moonlight. Then it occurred to me that there were people nearby and that they were talking in very low voices.

I looked round. There—a little distance away from the palm—sat two lovers. The man was in a blue gown, and the woman wore something darker. Suddenly the man rose, and as he started walking towards me I recognized him as Mallam Usuman.

"I will not fight with you," he said, with a wave of his giant arm. "You are no man. Still, it would have been good to quarter you before the eyes of the Chief Priest's daughter."

His words sent a hot wave of anger through me, and I knew he was lying about the Chief Priest's daughter.

"Draw!" I shouted and drew my sword.

He paid not the slightest attention to me, and I warned him: "Guard!"

But all chat Usuman did was to clap his hands contemptuously, and, from the ground around me, men sprang to their feet and ran towards me. I had fallen into a trap. With a mad thrust, I lunged at him, but he leapt aside, and the sword caught the folds of his gown. Next moment, someone knocked it out of my hands, and I was kicking and clawing to no avail.

"Take him to where he'll find peace. I'm tired of the wretch!"

They tied me hand and foot and took me into the town. These were very silent men; I could not guess from their dark faces where we were going until I saw the extremely high walls of the prison-yard. The horses stopped at the gate, and the men knocked and gained admittance. They handed me over to a short man who rubbed his hands as he let me into my cell, remarking as he barred and locked me in:

"You'll soon be all right! You'll soon be all right!"

And so, for the second time since first meeting Usuman, I found myself pacing a little room, and wasting my puny strength on the unbendable bars. I could not understand what power that man had in Mecca sufficient to make him so highly honoured and respected as to deprive me of my liberty. It appeared that he had a retinue of men guarding his life and the whole of the prison staff at his command.

I must have been in that prison two months, when one evening the Chief Warder called me and asked me if I knew Mallam Gobir. I said I did, that he had been my teacher for many years. He smiled and left.

A fortnight later, a woman called Dije came and demanded my release. She had an air of mystery about her that excited my imagination. She wore a black veil and good, and her gown scarcely rippled as she walked through the heart of the town. She led me to a large mud building and told me that I was to live there and teach her schoolchildren all that I had learnt from the great scholar. I was still a prisoner, but entirely under her supervision.

I welcomed the change with joy, partly because I was no longer suited to active life, but chiefly because it would give me a chance to fulfil my promise to Mallam Gobir.

The pupils were very willing and eager to learn all I taught them: but behind them all I always saw the mysterious Dije looking at me with a soft glance that sometimes made me think that she liked me. She was not beautiful. She couldn't be compared with

Zarah by any means. Where Zarah was tall and graceful, she was small and neat. Her voice was even smaller than she was, and very musical. There is little wonder that, in time, I asked her to become my wife.

This was not the hot love of youth, but the slow mature love of a man who has learned from life the valuable things. Looking back, I think my days in that school represent a very bright patch on an otherwise black field. The compound had that atmosphere of quiet which inspires the student. There were times when I forgot that I was at Mecca—a prisoner on parole. Punctually at dawn the pupils came in their white caps and white jumpers to learn what I had been privileged to hear from Mallam Gobir.

We had finished our work one afternoon, and the pupils were about to go home when one of the boys made a remark which wounded me very deeply.

"Mallam," he said, "if a man kills your wife, what is the right thing to do?"

"The right thing?" I stammered. Take him to the judge and he'll be punished. Why?"

"Nothing, Mallam. We were just arguing."

He sat down, and the rest of the boys' exchanged glances. The next remark was even less tactful:

"Please tell us about Kanemi, Prince of the Tuaregs."

"What do you want to know about him?"

"Had he a daughter?"

A mist began to gather before my eyes. These boys were torturing me. They had heard about Zarah and me. They wanted to prove it my watching my reactions. I stood still, trying to control my rising temper. And then it came: before my very eyes rose that picture of Zarah which had haunted me for so many years. There she was, lying amidst the debris, bleeding, her lips trembling as she breathed my name.

I could bear it no more.

I left the room. My heart was thumping hard against my ribs, and I felt choked with emotion. Tears burned in my eyes. Under the trees it was cool, and I stood there for a long time until Dije joined me, but though she tried to find out what had happened I told her nothing.

Next day, before dawn, I left the school compound without even saying good-bye to Dije.

One thing I did, though. As I was leaving the gate, I saw the school messenger on his way inside and stopped him. Impulsively I called him aside and took out a small *laya,* a talisman, and said to him:

"I am going on a journey, and I forgot this."

He took it from me and examined it. "Long may you live, but it is not mine."

"It is for Dije," I said. "I am in a hurry now and cannot go back. Kindly give it to her from me. Tell her, when the child comes, to hang this *laya* round its neck. It is a stong protection against evil which Mallam Gobir taught me. She will understand."

The messenger took it, and though his eyes were puzzled, he wished me a good journey. For some strange reason when I set off again, my heart felt much lighter.

THE CAMEROONS CAMPAIGN, 1916

I wish I had remained at that school. There is no doubt that I might, with Dije's help, have forgotten everything. She was kind, and gentle, and she did everything in her power to make me happy. Conditions were favourable for reading and meditation. But an impetuous man must always remain impetuous. Such little consolations cannot tie him down.

I remained in hiding at Mecca for about a month, trying to glean information about Mallam Usuman. Nobody knew anything about him. Somehow it didn't seem to make sense. He had been influential enough to send me to jail by a mere wave of his arm. Why did they not know him?

It was a long time before I discovered the answer. Usuman had changed his name in Mecca, but now he had returned to Nigeria. They spoke so highly of how little he cared for money that I was tempted to expose him. But no one would have believed me if I had told them that the glorious Usuman was nothing more than a first-class scoundrel.

This time, I did not find the crossing of the Great Desert such a pleasant thing as when Mallam Gobir had been my companion. I met a number of Arabs who were anxious to come to Kano for the purpose of buying slaves. Obviously, they did not know that the slave market had ceased to exist since the British had taken over the town, but I felt that such information would be better acquired by them when they got there. So, I offered to introduce them to the big slave dealers, and they gave me a passage in exchange.

The crossing took a very short time. My companions were anxious to get back to North Africa in time for the big Slave Market held once a year. As soon as we got to Birnin Kwoni in the north-west, I introduced them to one of Prince Kanemi's relations who happened to be there at the time and left them to work their own way into gaol.

I entered Nigeria on foot. Cautious enquiry failed to give me any clues about the whereabouts of Mallam Usuman. It seemed that he had vanished: or could he be at Mecca still? For a year or two I wandered about the North. I was almost distracted at that time. I had no home; I could not go back to Dije and her school because what I rightly deserved there was imprisonment. They had treated me as a man of culture and breeding, and I had let them down. Life was a torture then.

With a paralysed arm, making a living was difficult.

I tried to contact people whom I had known previously and made my way to Kano.

I remained there until the outbreak of the Great War in 1914. It was no use trying to enlist as an infantryman, because I could not fight. But the army was in great need of men who could work behind the lines. So once again I found myself in the army— in the Pioneer Corps. I knew too that with what Mallam Gobir had taught me I could help my fellow men a great deal. The soldiers came to me with all sorts of problems. I was able to help them quite often and my sincere faith and lack of fear gave them strength.

In the evenings we would meet in the barracks and tell stories of the Kano rising of 1903, and how much more of a man's fight it was than this thing they call the Great War. Why, men rode horses and fought with swords. There was no hiding in holes and taking potshots at unguarded men.

"I shall never forget one Mallam Usuman," said a middle-aged soldier. "Such a big man, and so fond of fighting."

"So, you knew him?" asked someone else.

"Knew him? Why, I fought by his side. He was a man."

The speaker smiled and looked round at the group.

"I wonder where Usuman is now," I said.

"Have you had dealings with him, too, Mallam?"

I smiled by way of an answer.

"Well, I can't answer that. But if I know Usuman, he's in this war of ours. Only, he doesn't happen to be in our particular company."

A prophetic statement!

About a year later I met Usuman. It was during the Cameroons Campaign. You may remember that the German Captain Von Reuben had occupied a hill in the Cameroons known as Mora Hill. It was our duty to take that hill and uproot the Germans from the Cameroons. When we went against them for the first time late in 1915, they beat us back. Von Reuben called his men "the heroic Germans". By early 1916, new troops joined us from the south, from French territory, and from Nigeria itself. The British General in command was much better equipped for the encounter. The result was that the "heroism" of Von Reuben's men ended in a fatal plunge down Mora Hill.

During this campaign, I met a learned Mallam attached to the French troops and we became very friendly.

"I've hear a lot of talk about you," he said. "I hear how very helpful you are to the soldiers. They say that you studied under Mallam Gobir."

"That is true," I admitted.

"He was a great man!" His voice was warm in praise. "How would you like to come with me to French territory east of the Nigerian border—to places like Fort Lamy, Mandara, Marua, and so on? That's where I live, and it's a happy place."

I said: "It would be very nice to go with you. But I haven't got permission----"

"Oh," he said. "That's an easy matter. I could get you a passport after the war."

When the campaign was over, we didn't leave the area at once. There was a kind of lull. Our troops were encamped on the hill and at night made a habit of going into the town for a little jollification. My new friend was not a man who liked such pastimes, being a scholar of some repute, but I count' always remain in his company, when I knew that by joining the other soldiers, I had a chance of meeting Usuman.

Under the pretext that I wanted to see the town, I took leave of the Mallam each evening. Within a week I knew every gambling-house in the neighborhood and who ran them. I chose a bar on a corner of the road, and went there night after night, and chatted with the soldiers.

One night I sat there in a corner where I commanded a view of the door. The soldiers came in in twos and threes. Their language was vulgar, and their behaviour even worse. It made me shudder; I was afraid someone might recognize me in these undignified surroundings.

The hour was past midnight, when a large man came in. My breath failed me as I recognized Mallam Usuman. The yellow light made a shadow of the cut on his cheek. As soon as he entered, he went straight to the proprietor, and stood talking to him in very low tones. Suddenly the proprietor jumped over the counter, and Usuman followed him. He opened a private door, and together they disappeared.

This was my moment. I glanced round. Nobody seemed to have noticed the incident. I drew my gown about me and stole quietly towards that door. In their haste, they had left it slightly ajar, and I quietly slid through. I pushed the door open and went in. The room was lit by one of those little clay lamps which send up smoke. Mallam Usuman appeared to be trying to sell the proprietor some contraband. He was urging him to pay up; in fact, blackmailing him.

"Usuman turned and saw me.

"Ilia!" he gasped. "What do you want, you dog?"

In a flash, he was upon me. His powerful hands closed around my wrist, and the knife I was holding clattered to the floor. We struggled for some time; then Usuman proceeded to strangle me. My throat was parched and dry. Lumps stick in it when I tried to swallow. Suddenly he relaxed, and I heard someone shout:

"What's going on here?"

The solder who had come in stood at the door, a rifle in his hands, the scared proprietor behind him. His bayonet glinted in the smoky haze.

Usuman, who was near the light, suddenly upset it, and for a moment the room was steeped in darkness. There was a spurt, a crack, and the soldier cursed. I had heard a crash and it dawned on me that Usuman must have escaped through the back door. I wormed my way in that direction, remembering the night of the *shanchi*, and had just gained it, when I heard a shout of: "Fire! . . . Fire!. . ."

True enough. The house was on fire. Usuman had set the place alight and had again escaped.

Another house broken up, I mused, as I regained the barracks.

3
DEATH IN THE TRAIN

I lost sight of Usuman again. After the war, my friend obtained for me the passport you are now holding and took me into French territory. My whole idea was to rest from active life, and to turn my attention to peaceful pursuits. I hoped one day to revisit Mecca. Every time I thought of Dije and the schoolchildren, I longed to go back to that city.

After a few years of a rather roving life, I finally settled in Fort Lamy, trading quietly and pursuing the studies begun with Mallam Gobir. I came back to Nigeria early in the 1930's and lived peacefully until World War II broke out. In spite of my age, I managed once again to get myself into the British Army. That was in 1940.

There is something fascinating about the army and fighting that I cannot quite understand. You make up your mind that you'll never fight again, but when you hear the bugle and the drumming, and see young blood in uniform, your own fire is lit, and everything ceases to matter save the desire to hold a rifle.

So, it was with me. I could not handle a rifle, but I could be with the boys, and watch them. We went to East Africa, we came back, and, while the others sailed to India and Burma, we who had already seen action remained in the country.

But everything has its end. I grew tired of army life. Late in 1947—that is, early in the month before I entered this train—I applied to be discharged from the army. This was easy enough, since I was old, and the war had been over for a long time. As you may gather, I had given up the whole idea of avenging Zarah. What I wanted was to go up to Kano, live peacefully for the few years left, and wait for the Great One to call me.

I boarded this train which is now carrying us. I felt the climate in the north bitterly cold. In fact, it was early this morning. I went into the restaurant car to ask for something hot to drink: I have a weakness for strong coffee. But there was no coffee, and I was told to go into the dining section where the white men had just finished a meal. There was a man there who they thought would bring me some.

I went. A big man had his back towards me, and he was cleaning tables and singing gently to himself.

"Greetings," I said, and he turned round.

I have never in all my life been more surprised. The shock was so great that for a moment every-thing went black before my eyes. I couldn't believe this. It was not true. To have been travelling round the African continent for so long without meeting Usuman and now to meet him face to face alone in a railway carriage. He was not much changed: he had put on a lot of weight, which was not surprising since the profession of trainsteward had brought plenty of food. His eyes had that softness which comes with age. His cracked lips trembled.

"Ilia…" he gasped.

"Yes," I said in a whisper. "It is I."

"Still alive?"

"Yes!"

"You're old now and feeble," he said.

"That we shall see."

As he spoke, he had begun to manoeuvre round the compartment. I watched him. When he came op-posite the door, I threw a knife at him, aiming to pin him against it, but he was out, and I followed him. For the first time in his life, I believe, Usuman made a wrong judgement. He had gone out—probably with the idea of escaping into another carriage—but the last coach in our train had no door into it: it was the goods van. We were both trapped: trapped in that narrow link between the two coaches. He could not go back into the restaurant car without pushing against me, and I could not move forward without facing him. One false step, and one of us would spin down the rails to be mangled by the roaring train. We stood there, looking at each other, that—whatever might have happened before—this was to be the end. I could see his eyes darting here and there for something with which he could defend himself.

Suddenly he rushed at me, and my foot shot forward and caught him in the stomach. He stopped like a car whose brakes have been suddenly jammed on.

He groaned, clutching at his stomach, and sank down on his knees.

I was surprised. There had been nothing in that kick —just a mere straightening of my old leg—and there lay Usuman, terror of the North, writhing and gasping with pain. For one desperate moment, his body lay wedged in the yawning aperture. When he realized that he might slip and be crushed to death, he tried to pull himself up by the sheer strength of his arm. I pressed forward to help him, but we were passing over a bridge, and with the jolting he hit his head on the metal upright. I heard him scream. He held on tight to me and tried to drag me down with him.

It was a terrible struggle. He held me in that death clutch, and I fought to draw back. The knife in my breastpocket dug into my side and was held there as we rocked with the motion of the train. You've seen the wound. When Usuman's body fell with a sudden crash down on to the bridge I must have fainted.

Frankly, I do not know how I got here. I do not know whether people have heard that the steward is missing.

My friend, I am going to die. It has been a hard life. But Zarah is avenged. I have only one regret, and that is: Allah has not thought it fit for me to see Dije again and explain myself, and to gaze upon the child she bore me.

EPILOGUE

T he old man was seized by a fit of coughing. Just as I was persuading him to rest and was putting away my notebook and pencil, he started suddenly and gasped.

"But the story is not ended. My child . . ." and his voice faded, and I could not make out his words.

"This child of yours," I said, after a few moments. "Was it a boy?"

He began to cough again, and to hold his side. For a moment, only the whites of his eyes showed.

"The p—poison," he panted.

"I'm sorry," was all I could say.

He lay quiet for a while, and I tried not to do anything that might shock him. When he was well enough again to look at me, I took courage to say:

"Mallam, I have heard your story. D'you think you could hear mine? Would you be interested in a man who was trained in Dije's school at Mecca?"

He looked at me as though determined to keep death at bay.

"I knew that woman Dije better than you can ever have known her."

"No!" he shouted, half rising.

"I know her better than you did, because you loved her as a husband loves his wife. But I—" the words stuck in my throat. I tried to say more, but my voice was thick, and that look in his eye frightened me.

"Go on!" he urged.

I was surprised at his energy.

"Look!" I said. I unbuttoned my jacket, so that he could see the *layas* around my waist. Each of them consisted of a little square wrapped in leather and attached to a loop. "Look," I said, and cut open one of the little squares.

He stared.

"Do you recognize it?" I asked him, showing him the square parchment, written over in Arabic.

"No," he protested, "it is impossible. Impossible!"

I paid no attention to him.

"Dije gave me that. She said you were a great Mallam and that you gave her that when the witches were worrying her."

"No!" he panted.

"She told me always to wear it: that if I ever met you and you doubted that I was her son, I should show you this and you would know at once."

"No!" he said.

I could see that he was saying "no" more from shock than from disbelief.

"Will you believe me, then, when I tell you that your wife, Dije, my own mother, is now at Jos waiting for me; and you?"

"Don't . . ." he whispered.

"We'll be at Jos in about an hour," I told him. "Then you can see for yourself. My mother is not as young as she was when you knew her at Mecca. But it—if you've not forgotten her . . ."

He was not coughing any more. He was not listening. His mouth hung open, and on his face was an expression that challenged the truth of my story. I leaned over to touch his body as the train took a curve, nearly spinning him from the seat. Then I realized that he was dead.

My eyes filled with tears. I covered his face with a cloth and prayed. I wished that I had never shocked him with my revelation.

We were travelling now very slowly, and I sat wrapped in my thoughts. A man had been standing over me; he had touched me three or four times on the shoulder, but I had paid no attention to him. Now he thrust a card right in front of my eyes and, apologizing, said, "Do not mind the offence, Mallam. I am Inspector Kofi, C.I.D."

I was not thinking then, and the words fell on deaf ears. "I shall have to ask you to accompany me when we get to Jos." The servile attitude he had feigned when he had been pestering me for a job was now gone and I now saw, in its place, authority. "I happen to have a special interest in this case, because I knew the late Usuman very well. Your late father's behavior aroused my suspicion, and I have been keeping him under observation for the last six hours."

I looked up at him and said nothing.

"We won't want much from you," he said. "Just a

few facts, since I see that you have a complete record of the Mallam's last words. They'll be useful to us."

My throat was dry. I moistened my lips, but there was nothing to say, and I said nothing.

When the train got to Jos, I handed over the notes I had made, and gave him the little blue book—the passport of Mallam Alhaji Ibrahim Ilia.

The sun was shining, and there was a group of little boys waiting to welcome Inspector Kofi near his official car. They were happy. They cared nothing about passports and vengeance and all the rest. Their life was before them.

"Step inside," said the inspector very civilly.

I got in, and the boys cheered as we drove away.

WORD LIST

Words are explained in the sense in which they are used in this story. This does not mean that there are no other senses. The list is not a substitute for a dictionary.

acquire: to obtain

adversary: a person who fights against an enemy; an opponent

alternative: another choice

ammunition: cartridges and bullets for guns

aperture: a hole, opening

assurance: anything, such as a promise, that makes you sure that something will happen

audience: a hearing, at which you listen to what a person has to say

avail: use (*to no avail means of no use*)

avenge: to see that the wrong done to a person is punished

barracks: the buildings in which soldiers live

barricade: a barrier

bayonet: a short, pointed, spear or dagger fixed to the end of a soldier's rifle

belie: to give a false picture of

betray: to give away (e.g. a person or a secret) to an enemy

billowing: blowing in the wind (or *waving*, like the *billows* of the sea)

blackmail: to use threats in order to make a person pay you money

blockade: to block, so that no one can pass

boredom: the feeling you have when you are *bored*, that is when you are sick and tired of having nothing to do
brandish: to wave something in your hand
bullying: forcing a weaker person do what you wish

callous: hard-hearted, unfeeling
canter: to tide a horse at a quick pace, between a trot and a gallop
cautious: careful
chaplet: a string of beads, on which a person can count the prayers he has said
clatter: to do something, or to fall, noisily
clawing: reaching out, tugging and scratching with your hands
clutch: to grab hold of firmly
clutter up: to collect or pile up, in an untidy and inconvenient way
cock (of a rifle): to make ready for firing
coherent: arranged in proper order
commission: to give a person a job to do
compartment: one of the parts of a railway coach in which passengers sit
confidential: entrusted with secrets, private
consciousness: the power to think and feel and move
conspicuous: noticeable, such that you cannot help seeing it
contemptuously: in a way that shows contempt, that is, revealing a very poor opinion of someone or something
contraband: goods whose sale is forbidden by the government, or which have been smuggled into the country
culture: the development of the mind, refinement, the power to love the beautiful

debris: odds and ends of rubbish, wreckage
decrepit: broken down, feeble

delicate: neatly and beautifully made
desperate: reckless, because you have almost given up hope
devout: pious, careful to do what your religion tells you
    is right
distracting: preventing you from paying attention to what
    is going on
duel: a fight between two persons

embroidery: decoration stitched on to cloth
emotional: showing emotion, that is, showing you are
    moved by a strong feeling in the mind or heart
enclosure: a place shut in by a fence or other barrier
encounter: a meeting, a fight
enormous: very big indeed
errand: a task which you go off to do for someone else
experience: what you have learnt by doing the same thing
    before

fanatic: a person who is filled with a wild fervour
fascinating: so interesting or attractive that you cannot
    give it up
fodder: food for horses
furiously: in a furious way, that is, wildly and savagely
fury: wild anger

gale: a strong wind
gallop: to ride a horse at a gallop, as fast as it will go
gesture: a movement of the hand or arm
glean: to gather carefully, to collect
Great Desert: the sandy wastes of the Sahara

Hammock: a bed of canvas or netting, hung by a rope at
    each end
Haversack: a canvas bag slung over the shoulder by a strap

Hero-worshipper: a person who *worships*, or is strongly attracted by, another because he thinks he is a great *hero*

Horde: a dense crowd of people

illumine: to light up, make bright or lively

imagination: the power to make an exciting picture in your mind

impatient: annoyed at being kept waiting

impetuously: without stopping to think

impulse: a sudden thought or wish

incident: something that has happened

inclination: a wish

infantry: soldiers who fight and march on foot

infantryman: a soldier who fights and marches on foot

influential: able to *influence* others, that is, make them do what you wish

innocent: not guilty

insignificant: of no importance

intone: to say, or chant, in a solemn tone

intrigue: to make a person wonder

intrusion: a rude interruption

investigation: an attempt to find out something

jocularly: jokingly, as a joke

jollification: a gay party

Juju Rock: a mysterious rock rising from the River Niger close to the Jebba railway bridge

liberty: freedom, the power to go where, and do what, you wish

litter: to scatter untidily about

livestock: animals (horses, cows, sheep, etc.) kept by men

looting: stealing from houses, especially in a village or
   town destroyed by war, earthquake, etc.

machine-gun: an automatic gun which fires a constant
   stream of bullets
Mallam: a scholar or teacher, especially of the Muslim
   religion
manoeuvre: to get yourself into the best position to do
   what you wish
meditate: to think and pray
meditation: thought, or thoughtful prayer
menacing: threatening
merchandise: the goods a merchant has for sale
misinterpret: to understand wrongly, give the wrong
   meaning to
moaning: a sad, low noise, like that of a person in pain
moisten: to wet slightly (here, with the tip of the tongue)
murderous: aimed at killing, or *murdering*, a person
mutilated: body cut apart
mysterious: wonderful in a way you cannot explain or
   understand

numb: without feeling

obnoxious: nasty
obviously: clearly, plainly
onslaught: charge
ornament: a jewel or other pretty thing worn by a person

pacify: to calm, soothe
panicky: frightened out of your life
parched: dry with thirst
parchment: sheepskin, cleaned, smoothed and prepared
   for writing on

parole: a promise: a prisoner on parole is one who is let out
   of jail for a time if he promises not to run away
pilgrimage: a journey to a holy or sacred place
plunder: to rob
poise: a beautiful way of standing or moving
precisely: exactly
pretender: a person who *pretends* to be, or tries to make you
   believe that he is what he is not
privilege: a special honour or benefit
probably: very likely (*possibly, probably,* and *certainly* are
   three steps towards being quite sure)
procession: a number of people following one another in
   line
propagate: to spread
the Prophet: the Prophet Mahommed
prophetic: saying what will happen in the future
proprietor: an owner
puny: feeble, very weak and small
purposeful: with some purpose to be achieved, and so
   worthwhile, determined

quarter: to cut up into four pieces

ravage: to spoil, destroy (here, to strike many people down
   with smallpox)
recent: having happened only a short time before
recklessness: rashness, as when you have no thought for
   danger
reins: the two leather straps with which a rider guides a
   horse
restaurant car: a railway-coach in which meals are served
retainer: a servant
retinue: a body of men accompanying and serving their
   master

revelation: the telling of great and important news
roving: wandering from place to place

scorching: burning hot
scoundrel: a wicked, worthless, man
senile: slavish, without dignity
shaggy: rough, long and untidy
simultaneous: happening at the same time
sinner: a person who offends you by doing wrong
sneer: to say in a tone of contempt
splintered: broken into jagged pieces
spurt: a sudden flash of flame, light, speed, etc.
stupor: a dazed feeling, as though you cannot feel or understand what has happened
suspicious: arousing *suspicion*, that is, making you feel that something must be wrong

tactlessly: without taking care not to upset or annoy another person by what you say or do
talisman: any little thing which is believed to bring good luck to its owner
tauntingly: in a cruel, mocking way
terrorize: to hold in *terror*, to frighten
thump: to beat heavily
torment: to hurt cruelly and on purpose
torture: making a person suffer pain in order to force him to do what you wish
transitional: changing
tremendous: very great
Tuaregs: Arabs of the Sahara, who follow the Muslim faith

unbeliever: a person who does not follow a religion, or here the faith of Islam *vengeance*: taking revenge, that is making a person who has wronged you suffer as you have

venture: to risk, to pluck up your courage to say or do something or go somewhere

vital: (of a part of the body) necessary for life, so that if it is damaged, you will die

volunteer: to offer your help without being asked

vulgar: coarse and uneducated

witch: a woman who is skilled in wicked magic

worm: to wriggle (like a *worm*)

wretch: a poor, unfortunate man

writhing: twisting your body to and fro

wild: excited or angry, so that you lose control of yourself

wrapper: a light covering worn loosely round the body

wriggle: to twist or jerk one's body or limbs (as a worm wriggles if you pick it up)

wrinkle: to sag or grow slack, so that it is no longer tight and smooth

About the Author

Cyprian Ekwensi was born in Nigeria in 1921, the son of a famed storyteller and elephant hunter. In early life, he worked as a forestry officer in Nigeria and as a pharmacist in Romford, Essex. On returning home, he wrote his first novel, *People of the City* (1954), which was one of the first Nigerian novels to be published internationally. *Jagua Nana*, his most famous book, appeared in 1961 and won the Dag Hammarskjöld prize in literature, though it was banned in schools and attacked by the church. Later in life, Ekwensi worked in broadcasting, politics, and as a pharmacist, while writing over forty books and scripts. He died in 2007. His works continue to appeal to readers all over the world.

OTHER BOOKS BY CYPRIAN EKWENSI

People of the City
The Drummer Boy
Jagua Nana
Burning Grass
An African Night's Entertainment
Beautiful Feathers
Survive the Peace
Masquerade Time
King for Ever!
Restless City and Christmas Gold
Glittering City